Pablo
THE DRUG LORD PANDA

Written by Estelle Maher
Illustrated by Lisa Williams

Copyright 2024 Winged Ribbon Publishing

ISBN 978-1-7396388-2-5

Published with the assistance of

Dedication

This book is dedicated to you as you are probably the only person who will read this bit!

Acknowledgements

I would like to thank the inventor of Prosecco without which this book may or may not have been better.

This book belongs to:

____

Someone with a sense of humour.

Meet Pablo the Panda.
His fur is black and white.
He used to live in China. Now locked in a zoo,

The zookeeper's a knobhead,
so Pablo bashed him with a rock.

Then robbed his keys and legged it.

Pablo got on the blower
and looked up
his dodgy mates.
Alan came to the office;
he used to be
one of the greats.

But now Alan, a Triad drug lord, was crappy at his job.

So Pablo shot his brains out.

Next on the list was Sid the Snake,
who is good at frightening men.
Big Dave the Gibbon got involved
and asked, 'What's this new job then?'
'There's a ship docked in Southampton
full of heroin and coke.
The captain will look the other way,
And so will the security bloke!'

So off they fucked in an ice cream van
with jam butties for everyone.
And Sid brought knock-off vodka,
which they mixed with Capri-Sun.

They soon arrived down at the port,
and met up with Bill and Kevin,
who tooled them up with fuck-off guns
and an AK-47.

They found the grown-up candy
in a box full to the brim.
'We're gonna be friggin' loaded,'
Pablo shouted with a grin.

But then they heard a whispering, and spotted men in cardies.
They even wore big rasta hats.

Kevin looked scared and shifty,
Pablo called him, 'A disgrace!'
Then pulled out his new shooter,
raining bullets in Kev's face.

The Yardies were stoned and cheeky,
and reached to grab their guns.
But Dave was too quick for them
and threw knives at the black-assed bums.
Screaming, crying in their pain,
the Yardies fled the scene.
'You're boss with knives,' said Sid the Snake.
Now Dave's called Wolverine.

With no more hassle after that,
the gang filled up the van.
They paid the captain by PayPal,
and a bung for the big, Black man.

'How much d'ya think all this is worth?'
Pablo asked maths-lover Bill.
With a simple calculation,
he concluded, 'Around two mill.'
Now Pablo wanted eighty per cent,
The high life he does hanker.
No one will argue with this bear.
No one's a silly wanker.

2,000,000
C +/- %
7 8 9 ÷
4 5 6 ×
1 2 3 -
0 . = +
KERCHING!

The van pulled up at Pablo's flat,
but the cops were bloody waiting.
They seized the drugs, and Pablo shouted,
'How fucking irritating!'
Mr. Munchy
POLICE

The gang were cuffed and sent to jail.
The keeper came from the zoo.

'The animals will welcome me.
They'll wonder where I've been.
Including that cute Silverback
named Heather, the Big Gay Queen.'

'So watch your back at feeding time,
I'll be whispering to Heather.
To fill your arse with his big cock,
greased up with Imperial Leather.'

'Your friends have gone,' the keeper said.
'It's a very different zoo.'

'They've all gone north to Chester
and they've taken your bamboo.'

Poor Pablo died of hunger.
But where are all the drugs?
They should be in the cop shop,
With the thieves, Tories and thugs.

But now there's a rich zookeeper.
His champagne is cold and fizzy.

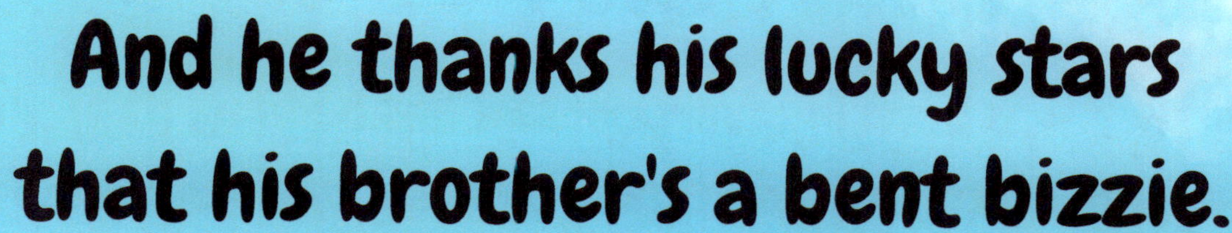

And he thanks his lucky stars
that his brother's a bent bizzie.

About the Author

Estelle Maher was born in Liverpool and has been writing since last Tuesday. However, she didn't get published until the Thursday.

Usually, she writes novels but thought she would have a crack at writing an adult picture book – the perfect companion for when you are sitting on the lav and waiting for toilet roll!

Estelle would like to point out that she does not encourage drug taking but taking Disprol or Night Nurse should be okay.

She also does not have a personal vendetta against the Yardies, Triads, Mafia or any other organised crime group. This includes the dodgy gang from the estate near her home who ride bikes that look too small and wear hoodies that look too big.

She also does not have any issues with pandas, especially ones that drive ice cream vans!

About the Illustrator

Lisa started doodling at just over a year old and she hasn't stopped since!

These days, the majority of her work is for children's books – think fluffy Easter bunnies and heartwarming tales with an underlying moral or educational message.

Like Estelle, she doesn't encourage drug taking—it's been a long time since she mixed with art students. She can take or leave vodka; however, Lisa would gladly welcome a gangster panda serving an array of ice creams. (Although the guy on Rhos Prom serves a very generous Mr Whippy, so Pablo would definitely need to up his game to match Shaun.)

Lisa is not aware that she's met any Yardies, Mafia or even Triads, but she is certain they all have a good side to them hidden somewhere.

8 10 Fun Facts About Pandas

1. There are identical twin pandas in the Peppa Pig series. What an easy gig for that illustrator eh?
2. Pandas fall out of trees a lot. You'd think they'd just learn to sleep in a bloody bed.
3. A panda can shit up to 40 times a day. The author nearly managed that on a trip to Egypt.
4. Pandas are good swimmers but have failed to qualify for the Olympics at the time of print.
5. Pandas think you are a perv if you watch them mate. Unlike gorillas (see page 21).
6. To stop phantom pregnancies in pandas, zookeepers give them weed brownies so they get so stoned they end up being not arsed about getting pregnant and just watch Big Brother instead.
7. A badger was arrested in Sheffield for impersonating a panda.
8. A panda who dances for visitors in a zoo in USA has had to apply for a green card to continue to work.